Thank you to the generous team who gave their time and talents to make this book possible:

Authors
Ellenore Angelidis
and Leyla Angelidis

Illustrator
Eyayu Genet

Creative Directors
Caroline Kurtz, Jane Kurtz,
and Kenny Rasmussen

Designer
Beth Crow

Ready Set Go Books, an Open Hearts Big Dreams Project

Copyright © 2022 Ready Set Go Books

ISBN: 979-8410806046
Library of Congress Control Number: 2022902183

All rights reserved. No part of this book may be reproduced, scanned or distributed in any printed or electronic form without permission.
Printed in Seattle, WA, U.S.A.

Publication Date: 2/8/2022

Surprise on Lake Tana!

Maajabu Ziwa Tana

English and Kiswahili

One day, a girl and her friend went to visit the girl's uncle near Lake Tana.

Siku moja, msichana na rafiki yake walienda kutembelea ami ya msichana karibu na Ziwa Tana.

They wanted to go by boat to an island to see an old, old church.

Wao walitaka kwenda kwa njia ya mashua katika kisiwa ili kuona kanisa zee, zee sana.

"Are you scared?" the girl's uncle asked.
"No," she said.

"Unaogopa?" ami ya msichana aliuliza.
"La," msichana alisema.

But the lake was big, and the boat was small.

Lakini ziwa lilikuwa kubwa, na mashua ilikuwa ndogo.

Soon, they saw a bird on a branch.

Muda baadaye, waliona ndege kwenye tawi.

Men were fishing from papyrus canoes.

Wanaume walikuwa wakivua samaki kutoka kwa mtumbwi wa papyrus.

Everyone was feeling happy.

Kila mtu alifurahia.

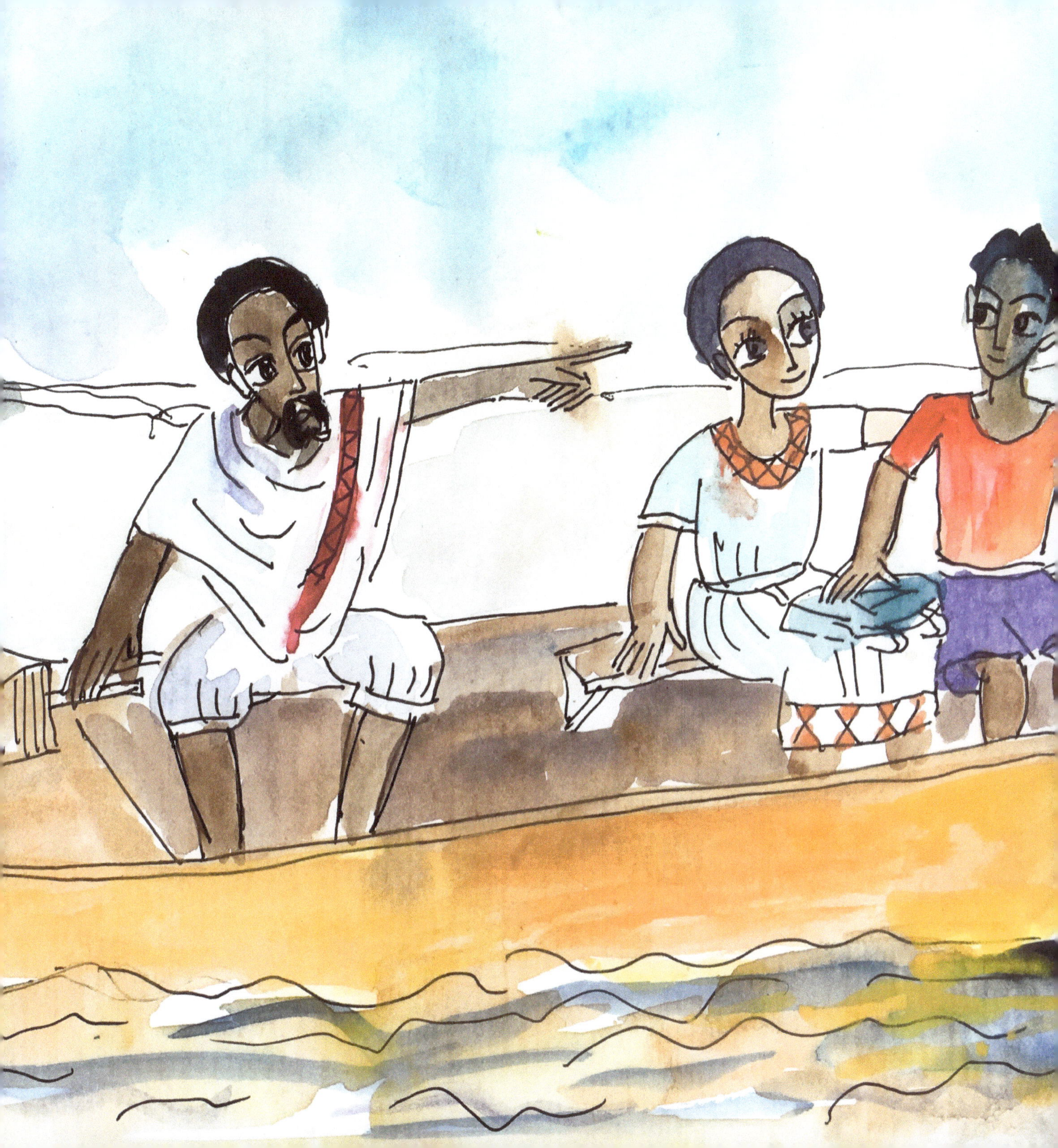

Suddenly, the boat stopped moving.

Ghafla, mashua iliacha kusonga.

Oh no!
Now everyone was silent.

Alaaa!
Kila mtu sasa alibakia kimya.

"I hope you are good swimmers," the uncle said. "Don't forget, hippos live in the lake."

"Ninafikiri kuwa mnaweza kuogelea," ami alisema. "Msisahau, viboko huishi ziwani."

Just then, two HUGE nostrils pushed above the water.

Wakati huo hue, pua mbili KUBWA zilitokea juu ya maji.

Now the two friends were scared.

Kwa sasa marafiki hawa wawili waliogopa.

The uncle laughed.

Ami alicheka.

He pulled a gas can from under the seat. "No worries," he said. "I need to fill up the tank."

Alivuta mkebe wa mafuta chini ya kiti. "Msijali," alisema. "Ninahitaji kujaza mafuta kwenye tangi."

The two friends cheered.

Marafiki hawa wawili walishangilia.

He said, "This is just a small boat and the lake is big."

Alisema, "Hii ni mashua ndogo na ziwa ni kubwa."

Soon they were seeing the old, old church.

Muda baadaye walikuwa wanaona kanisa lile zee, zee sana.

But all that day, the girl's uncle never stopped laughing to himself about his good trick.

Lakini siku hiyo yote, ami wa msichana hakuacha kujicheka kuhusiana na vile alivyowahadaa wawili wale.

About the Story

Lake Tana is the biggest lake in Ethiopia and the third largest lake in Africa. Its waters form the source of the Blue Nile River. Some of its islands are home to monasteries that are hundreds of years old and full of ancient paintings and treasures.

Ellenore Angelidis writes, "On our first trip back to Ethiopia with the whole family, we visited Bahir Dar where Leyla was born. One highlight planned was a boat trip on Lake Tana. We set out in the early morning in a very small boat for a family of five. When we were about halfway to our destination, an island towards the middle of the lake, the boat stopped. The operator provided no explanation and we all got a little anxious especially as we remembered this lake was home to hippos. It turned out the boat was too small to carry enough gas for the trip. So, the operator pulled a gas tank from under a seat and filled us up for the rest of the trip. We all laughed together in relief since the prospect of swimming was a daunting one. The next time we went my husband made sure we were on a boat that could get us all the way to the middle on one tank of gas."

About the Illustrator

Eyayu Genet is a visual artist and lecturer at Bahir Dar University. He completed an MFA at Addis Ababa University and has exhibited his work in Ethiopia and various other places including Qatar, the United States, Sweden, Equador, and Uganda. He has been awarded the Tana media award for his contributions to promote love and peace. He's engaged with many humanitarian and social programs and working to make Bahir Dar a showcase for art in Ethiopia.

About the Authors

Ellenore Angelidis is a public speaker, consultant, volunteer, lawyer, and aspiring writer. She stays busy with husband Michael and their three kids: two sons, Dimitri, Damian (who is an Open Hearts Big Dreams Junior Board member), and daughter, Leyla. Equalizing educational opportunities for children in Ethiopia is a passion that comes in part from being raised by two teacher parents and in part from raising an Ethiopian daughter. She founded and runs both OHBD and a new company L.E.A.D. (Lead Empower Activate Dream) LLC. Visiting Lake Tana and Bahir Dar has been a special highlight. Meeting and becoming friends with Eyayu Genet has led to amazing collaborations including three books. This is the first book where Eyayu Genet is also a co-author.

Leyla Marie Fasika Angelidis was born in Bahir Dar, Ethiopia and joined the Angelidis family in Seattle as an infant. She is currently in middle school and finds it unimaginable that some kids in her birth country don't get the chance to learn to read or go to school.

She has collaborated with her family to build a library in her birth town of Bahir Dar and to support other literacy projects through Open Hearts Big Dreams. She is an avid reader and aspiring writer. She has co-authored a number of OHBD Ready Set Go early reader books based on family experiences and personal interests. More recently, she is a featured spokesperson as well as helps with events and awareness building for OHBD literacy projects. Through these efforts she has learned more about her first country, language, and culture as well as positively contributed to her community in Ethiopia and in the US.

She has BIG DREAMS for herself and kids living in Ethiopia and all around the world.

About Open Hearts Big Dreams

Open Hearts Big Dreams Fund (OHBD) was founded by Ellenore Angelidis, inspired by her Ethiopian born daughter, Leyla Marie Fasika; both are key volunteers. OHBD is a United State 501(c)(3) not-for-profit organization that believes the chance to dream big dreams should not depend on where in the world you are born. Our mission is "Inspiring and empowering youth (K-14) to reimagine their futures by providing literacy, STEAM, and leadership opportunities."

OHBD harnesses the power of collaboration. We are made up of a small number of part-time paid staff and a large number of highly motivated volunteers with advanced skills, including artistic, editorial, translation, and high-tech expertise in Ethiopia, the Diaspora and globally. Our culture of innovation means we act fast on new ideas. Since 2017, we've produced more than 1000 bilingual, culturally appropriate early reader titles and a number of STEM and Model programs to increase literacy, inclusion, and leadership.

In Ethiopia, for Ethiopia; OHBD is based in the U.S. but we are committed to working with local content creators and to producing quality books in Ethiopia. Local opportunities and production builds local knowledge and capacity.

OPEN HEARTS BIG DREAMS

About OHBD Ready Set Go Books

Reading has the power to change lives, but many children and adults in Ethiopia cannot read. One reason is that Ethiopia doesn't have enough books in local languages to give people a chance to practice reading. Ready Set Go books wants to close that gap and open a world of ideas and possibilities for kids and their communities.

When you buy an OHBD-RSG book, you provide critical funding to create and distribute more books.

Learn more at: http://openheartsbigdreams.org/book-project/ or find all our books at: https://ohbd-rsgbooks.com

OHBD Proudly Prints in Ethiopia

OHBD developed our own local printing capacity and have a number of our books available to pick up in Addis. They are available for bulk purchase and we regularly donate to schools, libraries and local organizations serving kids. Please contact us at ellenore@openheartsbigdreams.org if interested in samples or ordering.

So far, we have printed and distributed (with collaborating organizations) hundreds of thousands of copies of our books in numerous languages in country.

Our goal is to get these books to all elementary students across Ethiopia.

About the Language

Kiswahili is a Bantu language and the native language of the Swahili people. It is a lingua franca of the African Great Lakes region and other parts of East and Southern Africa, including Tanzania, Uganda, Rwanda, Burundi, Kenya, some parts of Malawi, Somalia, Zambia, Mozambique, and the Democratic Republic of the Congo (DRC). Sixteen to twenty percent of Swahili vocabulary is Arabic loanwords, including the word swahili, from Arabic sawāḥilī, a plural adjectival form of an Arabic word meaning "of the coast".

The Arabic loanwords date from the contacts of Arabian traders with the Bantu inhabitants of the east coast of Africa over many centuries. Under Arab trade influence, Swahili emerged as a lingua franca used by Arab traders and Bantu peoples of the East African Coast. Swahili serves as a national language of the DRC, Kenya, Tanzania, and Uganda. Swahili is also one of the working languages of the African Union and of the Southern African Development Community.

OPEN HEARTS BIG DREAMS

100+ unique OHBD-RSG books available in over 20 languages!

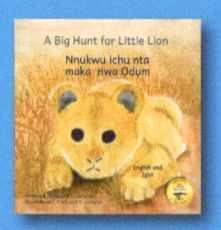

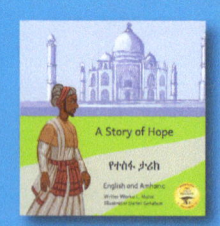

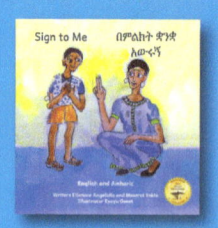

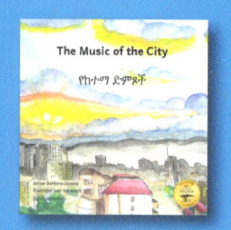

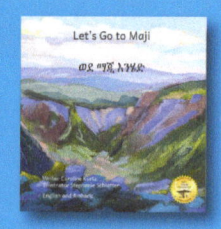

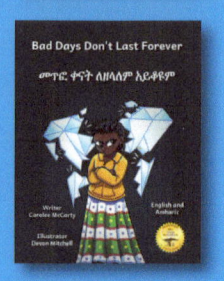

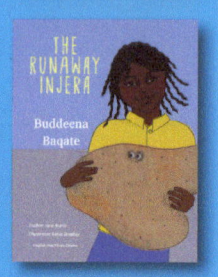

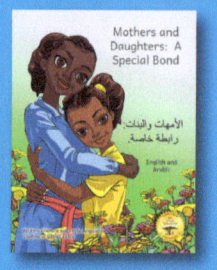

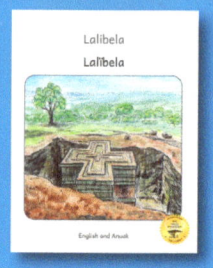

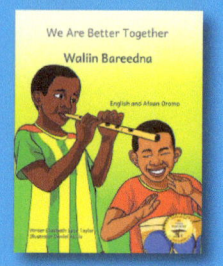

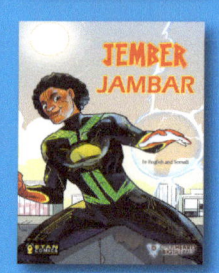

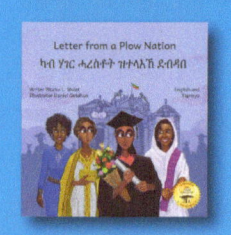

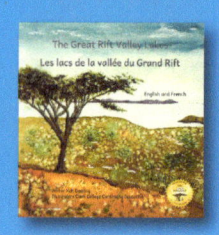

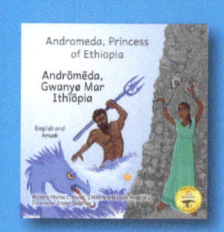

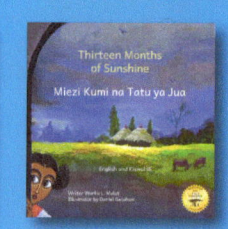

To view all available titles, go to https://ohbd-rsgbooks.com/shop or scan QR code

Open Heart Big Dreams is pleased to offer discounts for bulk orders, educators and organizations.

Contact ellenore@openheartsbigdreams.org for more information.